You

A Novel in Verse

A. T. Micalizzi

FROG DUCK PRODUCTIONS
Philadelphia

You: A Novel in Verse

By A. T. Micalizzi

Copyright © 2019 by A. T. Micalizzi, Frog Duck Productions

ISBN: 978-0-578-60403-9

For more about this author please visit https://www.instagram.com/poemsbymic/

1. Edited by: Andrew McFadyen-Ketchum
2. Cover by: Ronald Clarkson
3. Logo by Andrew Arcangeli
4. Line Editing by: Ed Carr

First edition. November 5, 2019.

to you:
for always.

Beautiful brown hair, blonde underneath
Perfect, pearly white teeth
Deep dark eyes that command attention
An angelic affection for all she mentions
I am falling in love with a stranger

If only I'd approach you,
        you would know my name
We'd be sharing our first date
        and nothing would be the same
Maybe I would steal a kiss
        or maybe just more of your time
Either way would blow my mind
        If only I'd approach you...

She walks around town so innocent and free
Every day I pass her on my way to work
Even if I didn't see her, I'd smell her citrus perfume

Today was different

She sat outside my store on the small brick wall
Drawing life's mysteries as they passed by

I couldn't stare any longer
My palms grew sweaty. My knees shook as I played over and over
How I was going to introduce myself

I didn't even know her name
Just her beautiful bright face
Her baby blue eyes glistened like a diamond
When they turned to look at me

She smiled so I smiled
We talked. We joked. We laughed.
All we shared was a common time. A place. An age.

The stars aligned for this meeting
We *must* meet again, I said
And she agreed

I took out my phone and she took out a pen
She grabbed my hand, jotted ten numbers on my palm
A special code that would turn a dream into reality

She etched her name on my hand and whispered, "Call me later."
The ink seeped into my bloodstream and straight into my heart
That said between thumps, "Your life is changed,
Your life is changed, Your life is changed."

I smile every time my phone lights up
Butterflies bang against my stomach every time I see her
When we walk together, it's as if we walk the world alone
Oh won't you please be my last first kiss?

She grabs my hand tight
Squeezes it with all her might
Rests her head on my shoulder
Whispers in my ear, "Move closer."
Is this love I'm feeling?

You stole my heart and won't give it back
But I don't want it back
I know it's in the best care
You won't let it endure something it couldn't bear
Just keep my heart in a safe place
A place where it will never break
At times, give it space but, please, no lies
Nurture my heart when it hurts
Gift it love unconditionally and it will shower you
With all the love it can possibly give
You're the only one I'm crazy about
You have my heart for as long as you please
All you have to do is keep on loving me.

You were in a red sundress, white Converse shoes, your hair curled down
We spent that day, and that summer, together from sunup to sundown
You'd find that perfect spot amongst the sand and the shells
I will always think of you when I smell those familiar beach smells

Whether on the boardwalk or under the covers
We sang our song of summer

Nothing was better than ice-cold drinks and our hot, tanned skin
We rode that old beach roller coaster and you had the biggest grin
We'd drive my Jeep with the top down and doors off
Blasting Luke Bryan until we reached my waterside loft

Whether with a cold beer or your rum runners
We sang our song of summer

Our nights were long and cool under the stars
Reminiscing over good times and crying over battle scars
We'd lay by the open fire for hours on end
Falling for each other in a way neither of us could comprehend

I picked my acoustic guitar while you were my leg-slapping drummer

We sang our song of summer

Those waves could only wash away our problems for so
long
Our lungs could only crow so many up-tempo songs
When the autumn wind came and the color of the leaves
all changed,
Nothing would ever be the same

But we'd always know we'd have each other
When we sang our song of summer

There's so much she wants to say to him
Like why she stays out late and spends less time at home
They never properly grieved
And now they live their lives alone

An unexpected hole was ripped into their family when her mother left them behind
The darkness of depression slowly consumed all light
Her dad spends his days working
To come home and drink away the night

She's cooped up inside her own head
Gravely scared to misstep
She sees only one option:
Runaway and leave him for dead

Haunted by pain
Yearning for a quick release
This high he feels is like his cane
Inching him closer to his final peace

Destined to relive his past
Forced to fight a losing battle against his demons
He chooses a bottle and some pills instead of mass
Why pray for forgiveness when life has no meaning?

Crying out for help into deaf ears
Longing for his suffering to end
Death is not what he fears
It's the broken heart of his daughter he'd leave behind
alone to mend

Will today be the last page of his book?
On the one hand, he'd end his family's strife
On the other, he could rewrite the chapters addiction
took
Will he decide if one more high is worth his life?

May the sun shine through your eyes
    I'll take the darkness.

May warmth pump through your body
    I'll take the cold.

May your heart be filled with love
    I'll take the heartbreak.

Her eyes are empty, her hands cold as ice
Each night, she cries, asking the unanswerable *Why?*

My hand has felt more like bondage to her
She needs escape

I remind her of a place she now hates
No longer feeling the happiness I used to create

Her life before she met me sealed our inevitable fate
I'm holding on by the skin of my teeth

I love her but I can't compete
With a life where she can breathe

Temptation lies on your soft lips
How much I crave just one kiss
Your eyes fixated opposite mine
Wishing the same, but with a different guy

He promises to give you a different life
Something I never could
I remind you of the town you despise
While he represents bluer skies

Rain trickled slowly down my windshield
If I stepped outside, would it hide my tears?
You pulled up next to me at one of our familiar spots
Like a drug dealer and a customer
I knew it was coming when you said "we need to talk"
You saw my pain, but it was time for you to leave this place
You said you'd be traveling to see your cousin
In California or your Aunt in Tennessee
But you never mentioned the guy you followed to San Jose
You packed your car so tight, you could barely squeeze in
With a quick goodbye and a kiss on the cheek
You drove out of our town and left me behind

She probably shone like a star in the crowd
You wanted nothing more in the world but a simple conversation
But talking won't last too long

Expect an adrenaline rush then doing something a little illegal
When night deepens, you'll hear every story about every constellation
She's a horrible texter so don't worry if she doesn't answer at first
She wants you to be present and in the moment, so take her out a lot

If you're special, she'll open her heart to you, and you'll see her at her worst
To get her through, just keep your ears open, kiss her, remind her
Every day how beautiful she is because she'll never tell herself

She'd rather spend time with you than receive a gift
Christmas is her favorite time, don't be surprised if she turns into an elf
But she makes the best of what every season brings
Remember to stop and pet every puppy
No, there's no other show she wants to watch more than "Friends"

Never forget how lucky you are

If you take her for granted, it will end
Whatever you do, shower her with all of the love you can give
Or you'll end up writing a letter to the guy who stole your girl

Click, scroll, shoot… there you are

Constant happiness is the social media disease
Eating away at my heart and my head
But I can't stop scrolling, even if
I unfollow you, I can't unsee you
Rather than go out and get over you, it's easier to

Click, scroll, shoot… there you are

Words are powerful
But sticks and stones are too

She was a cannibal
She bit my heart in two

She sucked the life out of me
Took advantage of what I was too blind to see

Told me what I couldn't be
And I believed her

Eternal sunshine
On a careless mind
Blissfully running through life
With no more than a dime
And a bottle of wine

Why does she have no strife?

Is it she that unlocked the secret to life?

Why do I lay in bed afraid of the light,
While she catches the wind just when the time is right?
I'm left to petrify

She moves effortlessly
But it takes me all of my might
An internal battle day and night
To tear down my demons
And relieve my woeful plight
As she enjoys the fruits of the world
I carry its weight forever on my shoulders
waiting for sunshine to brighten the darkness of my mind

I miss who I was with you.

Have you ever felt like everything you do is wrong?
Has the weight of the world rested on your shoulders?
Has the darkness filled your eyes and mind?
Has the joy been sucked out of your life?
Do you feel directionless and pointless?

When it storms, I never know which is worse:
The one raging outside
Or the one within

My brain is solitary confinement
It isolates me from the outside world
I try to scream for help but am silenced
By the demons that drown me

The nights full of horrors
The air is hard to breathe
The moon is my only company,
A glimmer of light impossible to reach
Will the Spring come in time
To warm my nearly frozen soul?

When you're at your lowest
And feel all alone, there's that friend
Who conquered their own fears
And lived to tell the tale
And now will help you conquer yours

Whether it's those long conversations about
TV shows, sports, the latest superhero movie,
Our biggest dream, the inescapable darkness
You must have that friend who's there
When you're at your best and your worst.

The thought of you slowly faded
So agonizing and painful
I decided rather than being jaded
To be grateful for all my youth
And the freedom losing you allowed

I found comfort in loud music, alcohol, strangers a few
times each week
Waking up with a headache in a foreign bed made me feel
alive
I became the guy in the town with a bit of mystique
I no longer was just trying to survive
Instead, I became who I wanted to be...

But when the neon lights went out, the madness
subsided, and I was all alone
I couldn't shake the emptiness in my soul
Being three sheets to the wind with a one night stand
Only masked the lack of purpose and feeling whole
Should I continue my reign as Mr. Mystique, I wondered,
or leap
Into the abyss of the unknown?

I denied help left and right
"Why would I accept something if my problems are fake?

It's not like a broken bone," I'd say
Though I'd have been in less pain if every bone were broken

I needed to take my mental health seriously
Without doing so, I would die

The strongest men in life
Are the ones who aren't ashamed to cry

So I sought out help at last
If I'm not happy, how can I ever find another

With the right treatment and support from my family
I recovered

I went from seeing the rest of my life from the inside of a straw
And re-woke, re-focused, re-motivated myself

I learned to love perfectly imperfect me
I took back every bit of life depression confiscated

Now I finally feel
Free

It's time I venture beyond my comfort zone
And experience the world
Find true beauty in all parts of life again
Find my purpose
Find my reason to live
For I am a speck of dust in a collection of unlimited stars
Yet it took a nearly impossible perfect storm to create me
Why should I settle for anything less than perfection?
It's time I find it

Step back and see the world from a different lens
Enjoy the small beauties
Reevaluate what made you tremble, what made you stress

Remember that by changing your view
You will learn to love your life
Most importantly, you will learn to love
You

Nothing flows easier than a stroke
Of my pen with beauty in my eyes
My heart fills with adrenaline after
Every word, every sentence, every page
I create characters, worlds, feelings, emotions, life
In a universe of chaos and death

My pen brings about a glimmer of hope
And pumps blood through my veins
My pen saved my life
Now I write to save others
For what is my existence
If I don't have a purpose?

Inspiration flows with the current of the Mississippi
Through the ruins of Ancient Egypt
Across the plains of Australia
In the smell of a French Bakery
On top of a skyscraper in Tokyo
In opera heard from an Italian Gondola
Among the stars scattered across the sky

The summer breeze washes my sorrows away
As the sun kisses my skin

My heart beats slow and steady as I sink between the waves
I'm surrounded by friends I'm yet to meet

Trying to beat the heat
I'm glad to be saved by summer's warm embrace

At an airport in Berlin on a breezy autumn day
Stood an angelic woman in a shirt that read, "USA"
Her eyes followed the majestic steel birds
While I couldn't take mine off hers
I found myself while traveling afar
Then found her at an airport bar

A military daughter; her life was the road
Luggage, different cities, temporary houses,
Her parents her humble abode
When life turned difficult, she'd run off alone
Distant lands with new people is the only therapy she
knows
A few drinks and an afternoon was all I cared to share
But sparks flew all around those uncomfortable metal
chairs

I talked about my life, my scrambled head, my broken
heart
She too was running from another relationship that fell
apart
I lost myself within her eyes
The way I did in the one-of-a-kind blue waters off the
coast of the Maldives
We were two lost souls hoping to find some peace
Now, I'm hopping on a plane with her to Greece

I found relief in running
Traveling to distant lands
Searching for myself
On the tallest mountains
The whitest sands
But as soon as I met her
Making the same great escape
I stopped running
And found what I was searching for
Redemption on her lips

I smell your perfume on her skin
I've been wondering how you've been
Even after knowing how our story ends
I'd do it all again

Life throws curveballs just like in baseball
When you're hitting home run after home run off
fastballs
You get used to consistency

Even if your experience
Tells you to look for the curve you don't

It only takes one pitch to knock you back down to reality
Turn a streak into a slump

One phone call flipped my world upside down
Sent me home in a rush feeling uncertain and depressed

All streaks and slumps end
I just hope I'm ready for the curveball next time

"There's been an accident,"
My dad's voice said on the other end
There was nothing anyone could do
Your Mom is dead

I dropped to my knees and started to scream
I gasped for air
I couldn't breathe
I went home immediately

I've spent time in Portugal, Vietnam, Uruguay
For a couple of years, I found every excuse to stay away
I was selfish and inconsiderate
I can't get back that time lost

She was my cheerleader, chef, teacher, and best friend
As her only child, I received all of her attention
She helped me create a future of my own invention
I will be forever grateful

It doesn't seem real
It doesn't seem fair
How could any just God
Take away such a woman without any care?

It's like you're still here
Your clothes hang in your closet
Your groceries sit in the fridge,
Your books lay on your bookshelf

That picture of you and I next to your bed speaks for
itself
Your love for me is everlasting
I want to lock myself up in my room
And let the darkness take me to you

But you wouldn't let me
You'd remind me how much I grew
And that you prepared me to succeed
No matter the bumps along the way

So tomorrow, when you bring me a sunny day
I will smile, I will reflect, I will be strong
Even if I can't see you, hear you, or feel you
Your love will forever light my path

She's here with me
Through the uncertainty and pain
Her life has always been the road
But she came home with me
I think this should become her home too

I turned down aisle five of the grocery store where I once
worked
Toward the back door where we used to get high, and
there you were

You looked up from the yogurt and into my soul
Your lips curled slowly into the most beautiful smile I've
ever seen

My heart sank into my throat and down into my stomach
As you approached to say

Hi.

Two letters never felt more meaningful
We exchanged pleasantries and a story or two

I wanted to take you out of that aisle and down memory
lane
Maybe it wasn't the place; maybe it wasn't the moment

A three-minute conversation ended with a hug
The chill from the fridges all around us was instantly
warmed

As you wrapped your arms around my body
And put your head on my chest

You looked at me and gave one more perfect smile
Before you turned and walked away

I no longer wanted to buy anything in my basket
I only wanted to buy more time

My life is a rollercoaster
I am only been a passenger along for the ride
Just when I was coming out of a dark tunnel
The path looked clear
I was reaching to take control
When you derailed me
What the hell do I do now?

One drink
A couple of hours
A few of our old songs on the jukebox
And some reminiscing

It's innocent
I just want to see how you are and what you've been up
to
Then I will go home to someone who loves me and
didn't leave me

You will go anywhere that's not here
One drink

How soft your hair felt as I ran my fingers through it
How smooth your skin felt as it rubbed against mine
How slow we moved to the beat of the music
How euphoric it felt to be with you

It felt better than we both cared to admit
I could still taste your lips: sweet rosé wine
Being held by you was therapeutic
Who would have guessed that something old could feel
so new?

But was it only for one night?
Will you still love me tomorrow?

I see your footprints walking up our stairs
To the bedroom we once shared
I smell your perfume on my pillowcase
My apologies wilting in a vase
I swear I'll be different if you come home to me

She was meaningless, that girl from before
I happened to bump into her at the store
It brought up old emotions and I was confused
I guess that's why I'm weeping the single man blues
But I swear I'll be different if you come home to me

Pictures of us all turned face down
When I was looking for myself, you were who I found
Only one mistake in almost a year of perfection
I was wrong to succumb to her affection
I swear I'll be different if you come home to me

Staring at the ceiling lost in a chess game between my
mind and heart
I saw her pretty face and I just fell apart
All emotions rushed back the moment I heard she was
back in town
I guess in the end, you turned out to be a long rebound
I swear I'll be different if she comes home to me

She and I went together like ice and summer.
We needed each other,
But in the end,
It was always going to be you.

It's been an eternity
But I'd have waited longer
To have you in my arms again

All the girls who came before you
Were stones on the path
That brought me back home

45

Sunlight radiates off her blonde hair
While her smile brightens the darkness

Her warm touch washes away my cares
Her assets rival that of any woman

She tells her stories through her eyes
The woman who conquered life

Text sent and 10 seconds turn into 10 minutes
10 days go by and still…no answer

I took my shot and missed
I never want to put myself out there again

Then, on day 11, I see you and fall in love
All over again and wonder,

Will I make the same mistake again
Again, and again?

You're the sweetest poison
You're going to kill me
I'm addicted to your taste
I can never get enough

Your hair looks lighter, your skin darker
Your hands still intertwine with mine
Your eyes have grown deeper, constantly wandering the distance
Though your heart still flutters for me

You excitedly explain your adventures, then your mind drifts away
You tell stories of our past as we lay under the stars as you move in closer
Your exotic outfits speak of the places you've been
But you still wear the necklace I first bought you

You often disappear and I don't see you for awhile
Then you spend days on end wanting nothing more than to be with me
When I talk about a future together, you ignore me, you run away
Then you tell me you love me

Is this our time
Or will I lose you again to the world?

Stay still
So I can live this moment forever.
When you leave me again, I'll always have a piece of you.
I'll remember how your eyes sparkled when you looked
into mine,
How your smile told me that I made you happy,
How your heart beat exclusively in love with me.
If only for this moment.

She was a free drifter with a full ride
High-speed chaser with a wild side
We took the long way home whenever we'd drive
Because time wasn't on our side

Every second I spend with you
Reminds me of what love truly is

Another adventure
Just you and me

We thought old thrills

Would bring back old feelings

How I longed to hold you
And never let you go

But as the sun set
Our adventures came to a close

I sit in silent crying, imagining your gaze
Only now I realize the error of my ways
I thought you were forever,
But my friends say you are a phase.
Little do they know, the path to your heart is a maze

You left me at a dead end, forever to remain
Scratching, climbing, clawing at your walls in pain
Still, the way your eyes sparkled
On your face unmade
Left my heart certain, we were meant to be for the rest of
our days

Rather than giving up, sorry or ashamed
I'm lacing back up the strings of my heart
I'm finding my way out of this labyrinth
Without shame.

I saw your face in the girl at the bar
I heard your voice in the beat of our favorite song in the car
I felt your presence underneath that old oak tree
Do you still think about me?

I saw your blue eyes in the waves of the ocean
I smelled the first time we met when I opened that familiar lotion
I tasted your lips with one sip of my cinnamon tea
Do you still think about me?

Your silhouette still appears on some random walls
I swear I see you laughing in a leaf pile each fall
I picture you every time I want to flee
Do you still think about me?

I spend each wakeless night traveling down memory lane
Not allowing my love for you to wane
Hoping for the slightest guarantee
That you still think about me

I stumbled into a bar about a mile from my home
To drink off Valentine's Day alone

I found a diversity of people in the dingy compound
An amusement park's lost and found

They each had a story, a reason they sat in their seats
Together we shared our misery in that sanctuary off Main
Street.

Bob was an old bartender who's been doing it for too
long
He doubled as a therapist every night since his wife
passed on

Jody was a lover who spent her nights working on the
street
For one night, she made men feel love, something she
never received

Jack sulked in the corner over his wife who lacked
remorse
Yesterday he caught her sleeping with his best friend,
today she wants a divorce

Mary miscarried her son and lost her husband's heart last
week
Barry was a heavyweight boxer who beat cancer but is
now too weak to compete

Dave fell in love with the bottle and out of love with his
girlfriend
Phil lost his friends in a foreign land he was forced to
defend

Everyone had a story but all found dates to help them
bounce back
So I introduced myself to Mary and found a seat among
the crew

She was an acquired taste but took away my blues
Out poured my stories, my darkness, my heart

All about one girl and the Valentine's Days we were
spending apart
The night went black and I awoke in my bed

No Mary, no bar, no patrons, no holiday
Just a pounding sensation in my head

I never found that bar nor saw those faces again
But it was clear I had to find you and make amends

After that night, I never felt truly alone
Knowing there are others living lives like cyclones

So when I take too many punches and life knocks me
down
I think of the night I spent in the Lost and Found

Year One was tough but eventful
I moved into an apartment I couldn't afford
With massive American debt
And settled for a copywriting job that didn't pay near enough
Because that's what was expected of me…right?
I never stopped writing

Year Two I played the field, but only thought about you
Swipe left, swipe right, swipe left, swipe right
Modern dating is a game of Love Roulette:
Match, message, unfulfilling sex, back to being alone
Is love meant to be found on an app?
I never stopped writing

Year Three was for me
I remembered life's lessons and took a leap of faith
I quit my job, invested solely in me, and my books
Started to sell, my career took off, and I became a household name
This is everything I've always wanted…right?
I never stopped dreaming

Year Four and thirty was knocking on the door
I've walked amongst the stars and onto every bookshelf in America
I paid off my debt, bought the perfect house, and took care of my loved ones
I've traveled the world, met powerful people, and found love

Still…Why do I still feel lonely?
I never stopped dreaming

When I see the wonders of the night sky
Billions of years of endless space
I realize how insignificant your problems are
And oh how insignificant the stars are
Compared to you

Late one night
I was visited by a friend
The same one who saved me
When I was ready for life to end

"Tonight," he said, "I decided to fly
I've always been scared to fail
Tonight, I took that leap
And the wind caught me just fine

I soared over my familiar, ugly town
I saw many familiar, ugly faces
So many memories returned
So much pain remembered

I decided to change direction to a land unknown
A cool breeze hit my face as I glided over glaciers
The sky lit with waves of glorious colors
The icy ground reflecting them in perfect tranquility

I drifted south to warmer air
I soared ever so slightly over the ocean leaving ripples in
my wake
The sun rose over the water, painting a portrait that could
only be painted by Mother Nature
The sand provided a perfect seat to view her magnificent
work

I continued my travels over lands beyond my wildest
imagination

I saw green hills topped with alluring flowers
Wild forests filled with life of all kinds living as one
Ruins of our ancestors; the world that once was
And skyscrapers reaching into the clouds; the world that will be
I saw a world of love, promise, and unity

Finally, I saw my familiar town and those familiar faces
Now, they aren't as ugly
It took seeing the beauty of the world to see the beauty in life, my life
But since I decided to fly, I will never see that beauty again."

And then he was gone.

The strongest fall the hardest
He doubled his pain and took on the struggles of others
Helping so many find their own way to recover
But lost to the toughest foe imaginable
Himself

I'll miss you, friend

When the darkness swallows a beacon of light
A little brightness dims in all of us
Second-guessing our decisions, our lifestyles, our futures
What our purpose truly is

In one fell swoop, I lost confidence
In myself, my future, my heart
As much as I try to pick myself up every time I fall
I could use a hand this time around

No swan songs will be sung
Just a few half-hearted eulogies will be written from a distance
And a great number of people saying, "I told you so," or "It was only a matter of time"
Those of us who are a bit broken are expected to die young

When a beacon of light is swallowed by the darkness
And we can no longer see their smile, touch their skin, hear their voice
All that is left is feeling their heart
Because their light will always shine in us

Autumn leaves covered the battered road
Daylight gave way to an evening moon
Your blue eyes as deep as a midnight sea
I stood longing to approach until fate intervened
We walked for *hours* with no destination
Our mouths barely moved but our hearts wouldn't stop speaking
We were the only two people on Earth
As we traveled down Bridgewater

Through winter snow and summer heat, our feet never slowed
Our private path always indicated we'd be together soon
There's still no place I'd rather be...
Lightning struck, a tree crashed down, and the road split in between
You slowly drifted away regardless of how much I pleaded
For a new path I never stopped seeking
But in your heart, there was a dearth of love
As we went our separate ways on Bridgewater

Over time, the road was mended and no evidence of damage showed on the surface
Through the rustling autumn leaves, a man walked hand in hand with the woman he hoped to swoon
As I pondered the cycle of life underneath a familiar pine tree
And pictured our memories like a movie scene
Down our path and towards me, you proceeded

No words, just a curl of your lips, and I felt one last
fleeting feeling
Like we were the only two people on Earth
As we walked down Bridgewater

Just as life beats me down
And I feel all alone in this empty town
When I'm battered, broken, and confused
You always come back around
To pick me up off of the cold hard ground
My one and only muse

So long it's been since I've seen your face
We've spent years and miles apart
But no matter where this crazy life took us
I have been in love with you

We're like two magnets
No matter how far you pull us apart,
When we're close, we're inseparable

We're two halves of a whole
One is incomplete
Without the other

I've crossed the Rocky Mountains
I'm swum through the Coral Reefs
I've marveled at the Trevi Fountain
I've walked Philly's cobblestone streets

I've met a lover in Denver
Who broke my heart in San Fran
We thought a few nights would turn into forever
Until I met forever's end

I've been so many places; I've experienced the world
Lonely as it may have been, I constantly stumbled across
one girl
Lost broken and confused, I did all I could do
And found my biggest adventure—my last road led to
you

I ventured through the Redwoods
Saw man conquer the stars
I've watched the moon as it eclipsed the sun
To show us just how small we are

I traveled down a distant path
One familiar, one free
When I reached the end of that
I found home, I found me

I've been to so many places; experienced the world
Lonely as it may have been, I constantly stumbled across
one girl

You helped me find myself, something even I could not do
I found my biggest adventure—my last road led to you

Hit after hit novel
Stories flow from my pen like water downriver
Since you've been back in my life
You inspire me to be more than I ever dreamed

You picked it out in a little shop while driving through Arizona
Only a day after we broke up
That tiny potted cactus was my namesake
It kept you sane when we were apart

It moved all over the country with you
The perfect pet for someone who can barely take care of herself
Little Kevin may not be too cuddly
But he reminded you of home

You kept my namesake from me when you first returned
Because you knew you'd need him when you left again
When you left on your next journey
Kevin was there to keep you level-headed

Lonely nights and soul-searching journeys, the little cactus remained by your side
It saw more of the world than most people in their lives and experienced every side of you
After hearing about my loss at home, you both came back to me
My gift from you: a little green cactus in its orange pot

I neither understood the importance of the gift nor heard the story
I was just happy you were home
Then you stayed
Not for the time being, but for good

As our relationship grew, that little cactus remained
When we found our perfect home, Kevin did too
Little did I know that when you gave me that little cactus
You gave me your heart

She laughs at all my stupid jokes
Sings at the top of her lungs to country music on the radio
Enjoys a glass of wine, maybe two, or three
Then can't stop giggling
I'm falling madly in love

She loves to fill our movie night with popcorn and a good nap
Tries to adopt every dog she sees
Loves to play a game or two then quits because she's losing
And makes the cutest face when she's frustrated
I'm falling madly in love

She gets excited over a good candle and the smell of coffee
A little chips and queso goes a long way
She spends a lot of time watching Hallmark and reality TV
But refuses to admit it
I'm falling madly in love

She makes my heart flutter every time I see her
Grabs my hand, pulls me in close, and never wants to let go
She brings my dreams to life and makes memories out of us
But never fails to love me unconditionally
I'm falling madly in love

We stepped off of the bus
And onto the walkway
To our favorite vacation spot
You turned back and looked at me
With the biggest smile I've ever seen
The morning sun shining above the river
As you leaned in close and kissed me
Your cheeks blushed and your eyes welled up
"I'm so happy to be here with you," you said
Those words left me frozen
No matter where life may take me
Or how big my dreams become
In that moment I knew I wanted
To spend the rest of my life with you
Before I caught up to you
I asked your dad if I could have your hand
Then, I told your brothers and uncle
You were excited to plan our vacation
I was excited to plan the rest of our lives

We always knew this day was coming
I always believed in us
Long nights spent apart
Led us back into each other's arms

Your heart should beat exclusively for me
Our lives forever traveling down the same path
Until we draw our last breath

My journey is full of mistakes and regret
All worth the pain for this moment
Reaching past my breaking point
Realizing there is so much love to be had was impossible
until I met
You

My life will be complete if
Every day I will wake to see your beautiful face

You are my past, my present, my future
I was lost until I found you
With you I have a home, a family, a partner, a best friend,
a full heart
With this ring, I ask you for your hand in marriage.

I take it strong
       you take it weak
I like it hot
       you like it warm
I keep mine black
       you make yours sweet
But we'll always drink
       from the same pot
Let's drink coffee together
       every morning of our lives

Last night you died in my dream
And it felt like my whole world was over

Even in my dreams you are everything
When we're old and our time on Earth is closing

I hope I go first
For I couldn't take a moment without you

Walk with me one more time
To the farthest corner of the room
Look out at all of our loved ones
Their smiling faces, belly laughs, pure joy

Take a deep breath with me
And soak it all in
Because tonight will be a blur
Of dancing, drinking, singing

Most importantly, remember
How we feel as our whole world
Celebrates us as we hold each other's hands
And embark on a life

Together

Loving you is

Giving you my leftover Chinese food no matter how much I crave it

Knowing every rom-com ever made because we've watched them a thousand times

Understanding the difference between a candle and a scented wallflower

Blasting your music on every car ride

Tucking you in when you are ill

Buying six different ice creams when it's your time of the month

Ordering food for you even if you aren't with me

Lending my shoulder to cry on when you're upset...even when it's with me

Giving up 75% of the king-sized bed and 100% of the blankets

Reminding you that you are the most beautiful girl in the world

Back and forth, back and forth, back and forth we go
On the merry-go-round of emotions
You're right, I'm wrong, I'm right, you're wrong
Does this argument still have a point?

Tears are shed, voices are loud, and I always manage to put my foot in my mouth
You storm out, I stomp after you, and we dance the lover's quarrel
Ten minutes feels like ten hours
Seriously, does this argument have a point?

Our eyes run dry and our mouths run out of words
We play an intense match of the waiting game
You break down and open your arms for a hug
I embrace you and apologize and you ask, "Did that argument have a point?"

You don't ask for diamond rings, designer clothes, or a necklace made of gold
Instead, you want a simple stuffed animal to add to your trove

On our first Valentine's Day
I searched for the most expensive gifts I thought would make you stay
Until I came across a black-and-white stuffed puppy with a heart on his nose
So I took a chance on that puppy, a special message, and a single rose

A panda, a gorilla, and numerous teddy bears
You still keep them all and treat them with care
It's the simplest of gifts between us two
That taught me that it doesn't take much to say I love you

My books stopped selling, I haven't published any work in over a year
I have to settle for an ordinary job. I spend every day staring
At a blank page hoping lightning will strike my pen in the corner
Of the same coffee shop. Nothing prepared me for the self-doubt, the heartbreak,
The despair as I burn the midnight oil doing something I hate.
Why can't I find success in my relationship and passion at the same time?

The moon came and went as the morning sun crept up on me quickly
So I returned home defeated once again. As soon as I opened the door,
Claws scraped against the hardwood floor and the sound approached
Louder and louder. Around the corner slid a fluffy golden four-legged puppy
With big brown eyes and an even bigger heart. I bent down and he jumped
In my arms as if we were old friends seeing each other for the first time in years.

Before I had the chance to look for you, my eye caught a little note
Around a bright red collar. "My name is Teddy," it read, and I

Am your new furry son…practice for your human son arriving in April."
I read it over and over aloud as my eyes filled with tears.
On cue, I looked up and into your deep blue eyes.

"At one point, I thought I lost you forever," I whispered into your ear
With your warm body held tightly to mine.
"Now you're stuck with me for the rest of eternity," you joked.
The words rattled around in my head all night.
I am starting a family with my first and last love.
The darkest nights always give way to the brightest days.

No matter how much you may change
No matter how different you look in the mirror
No matter what

You'll always be beautiful to me

Sometimes I feel sad, dark, and alone
Other times I can't be touched, prodded, I just want to be
on my own
Even when we don't kiss, I still feel your love

Every time I'm feeling "normal," we fit like a glove
I know I seem selfish and it's hard being with me
But I want you to know you are the greatest gift of my
life

"He didn't care," he lied
Maybe it was his male pride
But when he heard he was having a little boy, he cried
When he put his excitement aside
He thought, "Is he going to be like me?"

A few years and a few thousand diapers later
Dad became teacher, nurse, and waiter
But he knew his boy was destined for something greater
So he smiled, enjoyed every little moment, and constantly thanked his creator
For giving him a son who was going to be just like him

His younger years were eventful and fun
With a small glove and a baseball uniform on, his baseball career began
All of the accolades in his path and games he won
Paled in comparison to watching his son
"My son is just like me"

With age came independence
The more they did as a family, the tougher it was to get him to be in attendance
With best friends and a girlfriend, he had new dependents
But he knew he could always rely on his Dad…which he did more than once
There was no more wondering whether his son was like him

His son was grown and ready to move out

Father and son shed tears throughout
But Dad promised a new and stronger relationship would sprout
He knew his son would come home often
Because he was just like him

His girlfriend became his wife, and the son is now preparing to be a dad
I sit in the hospital waiting room worried, confused, and overly glad
My dad puts his hand on my shoulder and says, "Having a boy ain't too bad,
Because you are the greatest thing I've ever had"
When I held my son for the first time, I knew he was going to be just like us

I look at you
The same teenage dreamer
Adventure seeker
Heart-breaker
Free spirit
And I smile bigger than ever
Because nothing looks better on you
Than being a mother

Working hard becomes a hell of a lot harder when you're
caring for a child
We traded in hot and heavy for quick and mild
Squeezing in a movie and a bottle of wine on a Friday
night has become our new "wild"
The bathroom needs to be tiled
Our clean and dirty clothes constantly sit in a pile
But I love you and I love him
It is an even trade

One miracle becomes two, then three
We went from freely coming and going as we please
To barely having time to pee

One boy and two healthy girls, each rocking our world
I learned how to comb my daughter's knotty curls
My heart explodes when I see them in my mother's pearls

We taught them how to walk, how to talk, hopefully how
to behave
When times were tough, we did our best to show them
how to be brave
We weren't too strict—sometimes, when they wanted
something, we'd cave
Nothing brought me more joy than their coffee mug gift
with, "#1 Dad" engraved

One by one, each made their way to school
Playing in sports, attending clubs, and performing on
stage
Constant running around, being busy, and being
completely selfless was a big change
Over the years, it became increasingly harder to even
write a page

We have a new relationship as mom and dad
We're a bit more on edge, it takes less to make us mad
As a family, we have more than we've ever had
Take the good and the bad

We wouldn't trade in any of this for the world

Where is the passion?
Did our flame fade?
Stuck in a routine we wished for
And made

The Dogs are barking
The kids are crying
We're running on no sleep
Just as we think
We're through
Someone falls down with the flu
Another bill is past due
But as I'm losing my mind
I remember each time
That I always have you

I once walked amongst the stars
Revered across the world
Standing on every bookshelf proudly
What happened? What changed?

The future scares me
The clock is unpredictable
My finest hour
Is just as random
As my final second
So, I have to decide,
Do I carefully plan
My next minute?
Or do I fill it with 60 seconds
Of spontaneity?

When you're in a slump
And every pitch seems unhittable
Life has a funny way of cycling back around
And throwing an instant home run
All you have to do is swing

I took my dream job converting my most successful book
Into a major motion picture
Forced to work diligently all hours of the day
I left you at home to take care of a family without a say
Turning in your aspirations to be a house fixture

It's the happiest I've ever been in my life
I wrote with the most creative people
And met Hollywood's best
Came home a few hours a day to play dad without a
single protest
I didn't think once about your feelings

One job inevitably turned into multiple offers
And I accepted them without your opinion
Why would you mind if I could potentially make millions?
In the back of my mind, I knew you'd rather me
Just spend time with our son and daughters

I turned our marriage into a game and I was the winner
Ignoring the tears you cried at night
To simply avoid another fight
The one who loses sight of love is always the biggest
sinner
Losing this game was inevitable

The caged bird sings songs of freedom
Longing for what she once had
It's selfish to keep her here only because it makes me happy
When it only makes her sad

The beautiful young bird was joyful once
Glad to come and go as she pleased
She was full of love even when she decided to stay
But never imagined her wings would be seized

Time took away a bit of her brightness and beauty
But the cage snatched her spirit
I selfishly trapped her so I could keep all of my freedom
But it's time I let go of what I hold dearest

The caged bird sings songs of freedom
So, I opened the door and let her be free
It pained me more than anything I've done before
But she soared so beautifully

She runs
Not because she doesn't love me
But because she forgot how to love herself
And I forgot to appreciate her

We don't even talk anymore
Except for who's picking up and dropping off whom

You left me in this empty house
The one we crafted into our forever home

I can't write
I barely have the motivation to move

Since I met you
You were what got me out of bed

But since I took you for granted
We don't even talk

The ground thaws
New life begins to sprout
I feel the newly found warmth in my soul
Cut-out everything distracting me from my family

And shaped myself back into the man I used to be
Necessary Spring cleaning

I welcome the April showers because they mask my tears
But instead of May flowers
Will you bring her home to me?

I slouched over the bar lonely and confused
Until a young blonde snapped my neck
Perked me up and bought me more booze
I had a marriage and three kids to lose
But she felt like my muse

She was a writer same as I, searching for a story, just like
me
Paris, Rome, Los Angeles, most recently Tennessee
She traveled the world and was completely free
While I've been too good at just thinking about me

The drinks slid too smoothly down our throats
And my mind started to wander
She moved in close, ran her fingers through my hair, and
asked if I wanted her
I froze and walked away to ponder
Is this really me or did I create a monster?

I turned back to the woman with a big smile on my face
She pulled me in slowly and put her hands around my
waist
We sat silently in a long embrace
Until I turned to her and said "We might both be on the
same chase,
But I already found what I was looking for"

I keep playing it on repeat in my head
If I were lying for the last time in a bed
Would I want my last words to be anything but, I love you?

You started our little family
My furry four-legged son

We didn't understand each other at first
Yet you gave us unwavering affection

You were our cuddle buddy, our stress-reliever, our ball
Of energetic fun, a therapist, a partner-in-crime

When our kids came, you were their protector and
brother
You cured any heartaches with a paw on the hand and a
big wet kiss

You filled our house with dog hair and chewed up toys
But you filled our hearts with pure happiness

Even in your final moments
You brought our family back together

The world would be a better place
If it were as selfless and full of joy as you were

You may not be with us any longer
But you gave us enough memories and love to last us a
lifetime

Thank you for being the perfectly imperfect you
We will always love you, Teddy

You stole my heart and won't give it back
It's been all yours since the day we met

We've both experienced so much since then
Regardless of the ups and downs, I'd do every bit of it again
As long as it leads me back to you

There's nothing you and I can't get through
At times, I placed you on a mantle
In other moments, I left you alone with too much to handle
But I am nothing without you

We weren't created as two; our hearts beat as one
Our love has survived every single one of our mistakes

When life gets tough again, as it will
And we lose a bit of our youthful thrill
I'll remember the girl outside my store making her beautiful art
Who inked her number into my heart

I took you for granted
Because the chase has been over for so long
What I failed to remember
Is that the chase is only the beginning
Of a long and beautiful journey
I searched for that adrenaline rush
For that rollercoaster of emotions
In fame, power, and fortune
I preferred a star on Hollywood's
Walk of Fame over a walk down my own driveway
But my dream was and is always you
I met with powerful leaders
Drank with beautiful people,
And shared ideas with the biggest and brightest
None gave me the fulfillment
I get teaching my child to ride a bike,
Decorating for Christmas
Sharing a dance with you
From now on, I vow to continue
Our journey together
Because with you
Every day is better and more exciting
Than anything I see
When I close my eyes at night
My dream was and always is you

A rundown building next to the grocery store
I used to work in, smack-dab in the middle of the town
We took for granted that needs paint, a small kitchen,
Furniture, appliances, a sizable investment
We think is "just perfect"

Day and night we spend as a family turning this vacant building
Into our shop, months of hard work bringing us to a dream
We hardly knew we realized until we had:
Our very own coffee shop

Filling our walls with art you created from all over the world
On our bookshelves, I proudly display my novels
And some of my most inspirational authors
Behind the counters, our children will eventually learn the value of work

When we can, we'll take up the couch in the corner and sip coffee
You with your art notebook and me with my laptop
Doing what we love in a place of our creation, together

During the day, we talk to, serve coffee, and spend time
With the community we once tried running from
On most nights, our shop turns into a safe haven for those suffering
Whether it's AA, mental health awareness, or a variety of

workshops
We found a way to turn our struggles into triumphs

There is nothing more satisfying in the world
Than to give back to others

We found our purpose
We found our happiness
We found our dream

Dirty hands, tired feet, and a full heart
Is more valuable than
Expensive cars, a pocket full of green, a head full of greed

Every night you fall asleep before me
I lay next to you and smile
I kiss you on the head and drift asleep myself
Safe. Happy. Complete.

I'm thankful to hear you sing endless Christmas music
For the next month, taste Thanksgiving's turkey dinner
And share that extra glass of wine we really shouldn't
have
To watch my family enjoy each other's company, smell
The fifty-odd winter candles you scatter all over the
house,
And feel the warmth of the fireplace in the living room
As we all doze off after a full day as a family

Snowy skies
I see winter in your eyes
Snow falls on you and me
Together endlessly

It's getting cold out tonight
Stay with me all through the night
Until its light
I'll weather this storm with you

Snowy skies, let's lay by the fireplace
Until the flame dies, watching the snow fall
On the cars and the tree
Stopping the busy world peacefully

Move a little close, let's remind each other
Our love just grows as we get older
We may move a bit slower
But let's take advantage of what we have

Snowy skies
I see winter in your eyes
Snow falls on you and me
Together endlessly

May this moment last forever
Seared inside our brain
An ordinary day with the ones we love
Is a memory that shall always remain

You stole my heart the day you both were born
You've filled it with love every day since
One day, you will steal another man's heart
But before then, there are some things you must know

You don't walk in the shadows of men
You lead the pack
When you are left wondering if you are good enough
Remember you are invaluable

Wear what you want
Say what's on your mind
Fight for what you believe in
Never let anyone tell you that you can't

Don't just work for a company, own it
Vote and if you feel inclined, run
Administer the vaccine for the disease you cure
Accomplish more than any man or woman ever has

You are strong, independent, and powerful
Without you, life wouldn't exist
You will never be second-best in my heart so make sure
never to be in yours either
The world is yours to conquer

When you do
Because you will
Give back to those less fortunate
And uplift the next group of young girls to do the same

No matter what, I will be by your side humble, proud, and in awe

The halls sing the sweetest songs
The walls exude warmth regardless of the season,
The kitchen always smells of family
The dinner table tells the greatest stories

In summer, the yard brings the party
During winter, the fireplace brings heat
The fridge is always packin'
The clocks ready to strike 5 all hours of the day

Our closets, laundry room, pantry, and basement are
always full
The roof is steady
The foundation stable
The electricity working overtime like usual

The neighborhood teaches our kids the best lessons
The living room constantly reapplies the glue keeping us
all close together
After a long day, our bed hugs us until we're refreshed
And our address is the map that will forever bring us back
home

There will be a time when we miss all this
So, let's enjoy every second
Every day is its own adventure
In our blessed Home

We were kids when we first met
Living carefree without a single regret
Swiftly we moved from one adventure to the next
With our days far from complex
But when the wind blew…

We were starting our lives together
Picking out colors for the walls, matching dishware, and deciding between cushioned or leather
Eating out, taking trips, and living free
All we needed was you and me
But when the wind blew again...

Our family started to grow with a fluffy puppy and a young son
We traded our freedom in for a new type of fun
Dirty diapers, constant crying, and very long nights
Nothing made us happier than being parents, so we looked forward to life's next delights
But when the wind blew again…

We had a total of three
Far removed from just you and me
Constant mayhem between school events, sports games, and growing pains
The love and joy we shared as a family is something we couldn't explain
But when the wind blew again…

Our little kids were grown and ready to move out

New lives and futures for them began to sprout
One by one, they found their purpose
They proved every parenting victory and mistake well worth it
But when the wind blew again...

We were in the autumn of our years
Our freedom magically reappeared
Once again, just you and I
Until we took on a new role, the name grandpa still puts a tear in my eye
But when the wind blew again...

Our family and hearts are fuller than ever
We may be old, but we still have more endeavors
Time moved fast but we danced alongside without missing a beat
We're still light on our feet
Ready for when the wind blows again

Our lives fit as perfect
As your hand in mine
As warm as an open fire on a cool fall night
As sweet as the smell of pumpkin pie in the oven
As satisfying as a fresh apple picked from an orchard
As exciting and unpredictable as the start of the football season
As relaxing as a hot cup of coffee on a cool morning swinging on our porch
The autumn of our years

You've been feeling sick for quite some time
We thought it was just age, that with rest, you'd be fine
A checkup or quick MRI became part of our daily routine
But this time, the doctor froze when he saw the CAT
scan screen

Then the doctor sorrowfully said those deadly three
words, "You have cancer"
I needed to be your strength...I needed to be hopeful...
But the doctor looked down in complete despair
Her body lit up like a Christmas tree—the cancer was
everywhere

We brought all the kids over at once and caught them by
surprise
Saying it aloud made it so real, there wasn't a single dry
eye
No one knew how to respond other than to share in each
other's love
And hope for some help from someone above

We had a great day with our family, we were all together
again
But as soon as we were alone, I could no longer pretend
I was frightened about your future, my heart was ready to
burst
Unfortunately, this day would be far from the worst

We held each other tight and cried
We basked in each other's arms until hours went by

"I will fight," you whispered in my ear
"For right now, let's just live in the moment"

And from that second on
We cherished every little piece of our lives

Fear knows no colors
Sweating profusely in a cold room
Eyes teetering between life and shutting forever
The only sound heard, the collective heavy beating of hearts
No one sure of what tomorrow holds

But

All savoring every bit of that moment
Different faces showing the same emotions
Shared tears and hands held tightly
Fighting the good fight together with family and strangers alike
Love knows no colors either

Your hair is in patches
Skin pale, covered in cuts
Eyes sunken and often closed
Your body terribly frail
You've never looked more beautiful

We're running against a clock with no hands
Let's just hope we find a way to add more time
Before it strikes one final midnight

"When you're sitting on our porch
On our favorite rocking chair
Watching the sun say goodnight to the moon

Look back up into the stars
The same ones I'd spend hours gazing at
But seemed so insignificant to you

Find the biggest and the brightest
And smile
Because even if I may not be next to you

I will always be with you
Bringing light to your life"

Crowds of people everywhere
Children laughing without a care
Christmas spirits in the air
All I want is you

In our youth we'd gallop through the streets
Sing Christmas carols for all to hear
Wish a Merry Christmas to all we met
All I wanted was you

We decorated the tree on Christmas Eve
Celebrated away with our family
I got down on one knee and said
All I want is you

A few years later our baby boy kept us up all night
I snuck down the stairs to fill the tree with Santa's delights
You kept him in your arms and sang him Christmas lullabies
As you both slept, I kissed your forehead and whispered
All I want is you

As our home became fuller so did our love of Christmas
The kids gathered around to hear you tell your stories and go over their wish lists
I admired from a distance and thought, "One day, I'm going to miss this"
I sat down next to you and you asked, "What do you want for Christmas?"

All I want is you

Our kids moved away and started families of their own
They visit on Christmas Eve but can't stay for long
As they left you turned to me with tears in your eyes and
said,
"All I want for Christmas is our babies back" and I said
back lovingly
All I want is you

In the hospital room, I sat anxiously
A little tree in the corner to spread some cheer
I kissed you on the forehead and whispered, "The family
is all here"
You looked me in the eyes and cried one last goodbye,
All I want is you
This Christmas Eve all the kids returned
They told their children stories just as you would
Our granddaughter asked me, "Grandpa, what do you
want for Christmas?"
I placed her on my knee, kissed her forehead, and said,
All I want is you

I go to bed wishing you were next to me
But when I close my eyes
You meet me in my dreams
And away we go to a place only we know

There you stand with your arms open wide
Reaching out for me
The light shining in your eyes
A smile on your face
And away we go to a place only we know

The pain goes away when I see your image
And again, you're by my side
Every morning I wake up wishing you were next to me
But I know that at night I'll see you in my dreams
And away we go to a place only we know

My pen is dry
No words no rhymes no phrases left
Only a lifetime of memories
A lifetime of love

I hope you're up there exploring the vast unknown
But when my time has come
And my story is complete
I hope you're done running

And will return home to me

Remember me not
For what I did
For who I met
For what I wrote
For where I've been
For how much money I made
But for the lives I've touched
For the love I've shared

You gave me everything I needed
Butterflies in my stomach
Heartbreak in the chest
Failure in the knees
Happiness in the gut
Success in the heart
Family in my home
Life in my bones
Love all my life
Together, we conquered the world
Now, I'm ready to do the same in the next one with you

A lonely old poet sits at the end of the Earth
Lost in time with his thoughts

A sonnet lies in the depths of his heart
The most beautiful no one has heard

The poet was once a simple man's son
Lost in the world with no direction

Constantly fighting his own reflection
Scared to open himself to anyone

The sun glistened off her hair like a sign from above
With her the poet found his home, his life, his voice

He knew he had no choice
But to throw all else away and bask in the blanket of her
love

Limericks, haikus, and sonnets of sorts poured from his
pen
As beauty surrounded his world

A house, a dog, a boy, and two girls
But nothing inspired the poet more than the time with
her he'd spend

The poet and she grew old in love, in life
His hand moved slower and uncertain, but she never
looked more beautiful

First her mind, then her body, as God gave her a cue to let go
Her spirit departed as his pen screamed with sorrow at the loss of his wife

The poet's days dragged on as he eagerly awaited each night
Yet every time he closed his eyes, a new adventure with her awaited

The sun, the grass, and the trees slowly faded
As he spilled every last drop of ink to articulate his internal fight

A lonely old poet sits at the end of the Earth
Ready for an eternity of adventures amongst the stars with his lost wife

A sonnet he brings from the depths of his heart
The most beautiful only she has heard

To my amazing family who has stuck by me no matter what. To my wife for her never-ending love and support. To my friends who continue to push me to be better than I was the day before. To all bedroom poets scared to show the world their work, thank you for being able to relate – you can do it too. A special thank you to my editor, Andrew McFadyen-Ketchum, SpettaDesigns (Ron Clarkson) for the fantastic cover, Andrew Arcangeli for the logo, and Ed Carr for all of his help during the early stages of the book.

A. T. is the author of the addiction memoir, "Too Far Gone" and "You: A Novel in Verse." He is also a poet, Social Studies teacher, softball coach, mental health advocate, and movie aficionado. He works with foundations to raise money and awareness for those suffering any number of addictions. He releases his short stories, movie reviews, and poetry on his rapidly growing Instagram page:

https://www.instagram.com/poemsbymic He is currently working on, "Far Gone," his sequel to his memoir, and a number of other creative pursuits he looks forward to publishing soon.

www.ingramcontent.com/pod-product-compliance
Lightning Source LLC
Chambersburg PA
CBHW030537130626
46552CB00006B/2298